W9-BNO-441

John Himmelman

Floaty

Henry Holt and Company
NEW YORK

Henry Holt and Company, *Publishers since 1866*
Henry Holt® is a registered trademark of Macmillan Publishing Group, LLC.
175 Fifth Avenue, New York, New York 10010
mackids.com

Copyright © 2018 by John Himmelman

Library of Congress Cataloging-in-Publication Data is available.
ISBN 978-1-250-12805-8

Our books may be purchased in bulk for promotional, educational, or business use.
Please contact your local bookseller or the Macmillan Corporate and Premium Sales Department at
(800) 221-7945 ext. 5442 or by e-mail at MacmillanSpecialMarkets@macmillan.com.

First Edition—2018 / Designed by Carol Ly
Printed in China by RR Donnelley Asia Printing Solutions Ltd., Dongguan City, Guangdong Province

1 3 5 7 9 10 8 6 4 2

For Jimmy, who doesn't float—
but jumps real high!

Mr. Raisin lived alone in a little house.
Inside that little house, he loved to sew.

Mr. Raisin didn't like anything else. Only sewing.

One morning, he found a basket at his front door.
It had a note attached that read,
"All yours! Too much trouble! Good luck!"

Mr. Raisin brought the
basket inside.

It was empty.

"**Wiff,**" said something from above. Mr. Raisin looked up.

A puppy was stuck to the ceiling!

"Get down from there!" shouted Mr. Raisin.

He nudged the dog with his broom.

The dog slid across the ceiling and into the other room.

Mr. Raisin climbed onto a chair and grabbed the dog.
"Outside with you," he said. He opened the door.
He was about to let the dog go, but he stopped.

"You'll just float away, won't you?"
Mr. Raisin brought the dog inside.

"This doesn't mean you're staying," he said to the dog.
"But I guess dogs need to eat—even annoying ceiling dogs."

He put a bowl of cornflakes on the floor.

"Wiff," said the dog from the ceiling.

"Oh, you can't come down."

Mr. Raisin tossed the cornflakes one at a time into the air.

"You probably need water, too," he said.

The dog floated to the front door.

"**Wiff,**" he barked.

"**Blah,**" complained Mr. Raisin.
"I have to take you for a walk, too?"

"Funny balloon," said Agnes Withers.

"Not a balloon. A dog," barked Mr. Raisin.

"Your kite needs a longer tail," said Mr. Poots.

"Not a kite. A dog," grunted Mr. Raisin.

He went
back inside.

Mr. Raisin wasn't used to having company,
but the dog stayed out of his way—most of the time.

At night, he was a terrible blanket hog.

But as time went by, Mr. Raisin thought less and less
about getting rid of the dog.

"I guess you will need a name," he said.

"I will call you . . . Floaty."

Mr. Raisin chuckled at the silly name. He hardly ever chuckled.

One morning when they were
out for a walk, the leash snapped.

Floaty floated away.

As Floaty disappeared into the clouds,
Mr. Raisin realized how much he loved his dog.

Floaty floated for days and nights.

Back at home,
Mr. Raisin sent up
balloons carrying
food, in case his
dog floated by.

The food never found Floaty, but he didn't go hungry.

Mr. Raisin moved to his roof.

He searched the skies day and night for his little dog.

Floaty floated farther

and farther away.

Mr. Raisin climbed down
from the roof.

Floaty dreamed about home.

Mr. Raisin sat in his chair

and sewed.

Just then, a voice called from overhead.

"Up here, Floaty!"

Mr. Raisin lowered his
freshly sewn hot-air balloon
and scooped up his dog.